GRUMPY GROUNDHOG

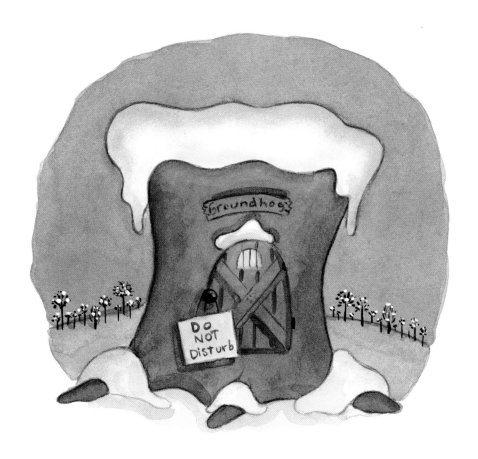

MAUREEN WRIGHT   Illustrated by AMANDA HALEY

two lions

With love to the twins from Punxsutawney,
Celeste Gigliotti Rombold and Teresa Gigliotti Smith—M.W.

To Mayzie—A.H.

The mayor stood before Groundhog's door
and heard a rumbly, tumbly snore.
"Groundhog," he said, "you're sleeping late.
This is *NO* time to hibernate!"

The people added with a shout,
"IT'S GROUNDHOG DAY. *PLEASE* COME OUT!"

The mayor pleaded, "I'll ask once more . . .

. . . won't you open up this door?
Please come out and greet your friends.
Groundhog Day is here again!"

"I won't come out!" the groundhog said.
"I'm closing my eyes and staying in bed."

"I have an idea!" said a boy in the crowd.
He stepped to the front and spoke up loud.
"Give him a paper to read in bed!"
"That's it!" said the mayor, nodding his head.

Groundhog opened his sleepy eyes.
The Morning Times was a nice surprise!

The groundhog took a very long time
reading the paper, line by line.

The people in town said with a shout,

The mayor dropped to his knobby knees
and begged the groundhog, "Come out, please."

"I won't come out!" the groundhog said.
"I'm staying in here until I am fed."

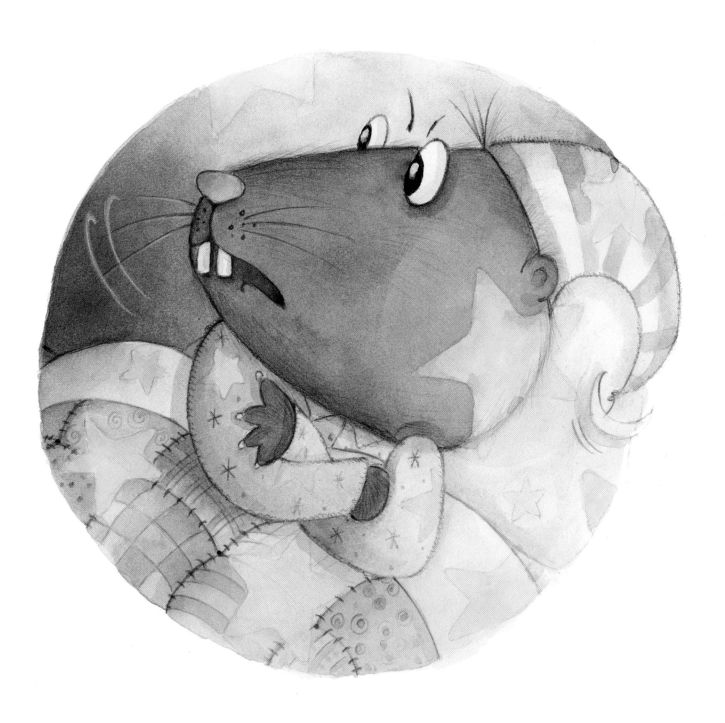

"I know what to do!" a little girl said.
"Give the groundhog breakfast in bed!"

They served him food on a fancy tray . . .
coffee and toast and a flower bouquet.

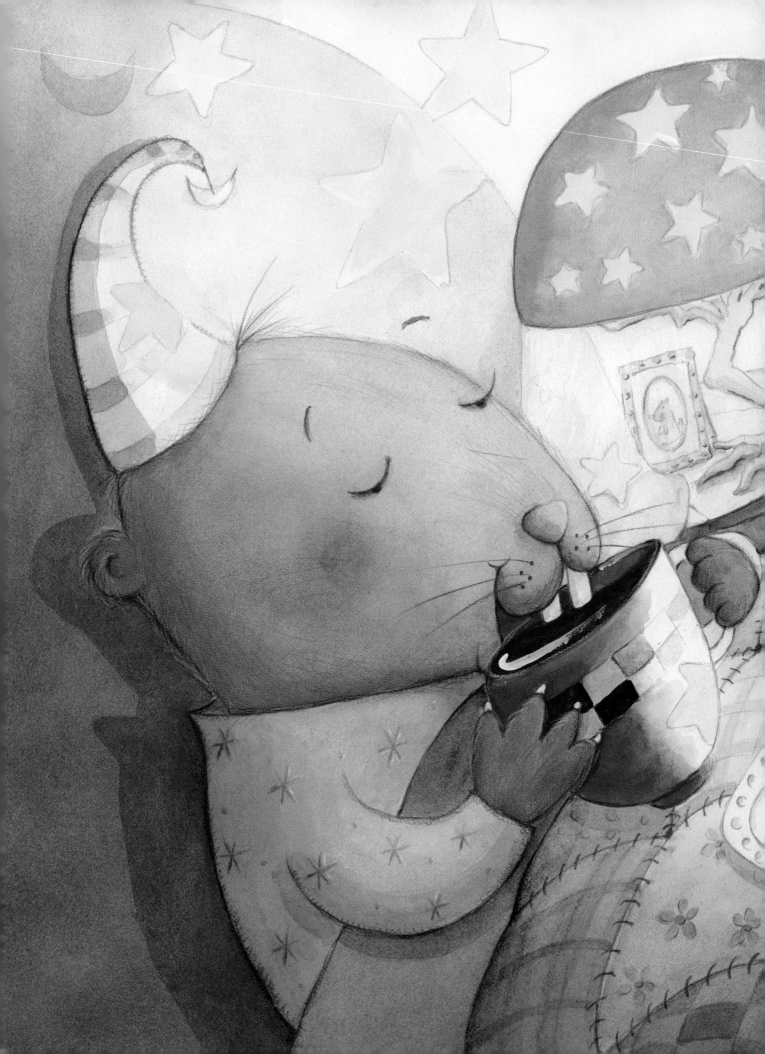

Groundhog poured coffee from the pot.
"This coffee is good. It's nice and hot."

The people in town said with a shout,
"IT'S GROUNDHOG DAY. PLEASE COME OUT!"

"I won't come out!" the groundhog said.
"It's nice and warm in my cozy bed."

A girl yelled, "Get him slippers to wear!
His bedroom floor is chilly in there."

"Of course!" said the mayor. "Find him a pair!
His little tootsies are cold and bare."

Groundhog never had slippers before!
He did a jig all the way to the door.

He twirled and shouted, "Look at me!

I'll step outside on the count of three."

The crowd yelled,

"ONE-TWO-THREE! COME OUT!"

"TA-DAH!" he said, looking about.

He blinked from the lights and the camera's glare.
A child said, "Give him sunglasses to wear!"

"HOORAY!" said the mayor. "No shadow today!
The chilly weather is going away!"
The groundhog said, "It's a wonderful day!
I'll ask the children if they want to play."

"Let's make a snowman!" the children cried.

Groundhog had fun being outside!

They made a snowman, round and fat.
It looked very nice in the mayor's hat.

At the end of the day the groundhog said,
"It's time for me to go back to bed.
I had a fun day with all my friends.
When spring comes early, I'll see them again!"

Amazon Publishing
Attn: Amazon Children's Publishing
P.O. Box 400818
Las Vegas, NV 89140
www.amazon.com/amazonchildrenspublishing

Library of Congress Cataloging-in-Publication Data
is available upon request.

ISBN-13: 9781477847053 (hardcover)
ISBN-10: 1477847057 (hardcover)

ISBN-13: 9781477897058 (ebook)
ISBN-10: 1477897054 (ebook)

Book design by Abby Kuperstock
Editor: Margery Cuyler

Printed in China (R)
First edition
10 9 8 7 6 5 4 3 2 1